For Bean, for being the best mum any child could ask for

Chops

and the Cat Burglar

Written and illustrated
by Matthew Jenkins

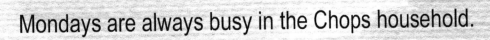

Mondays are always busy in the Chops household.

First there is waking up, which is always hard to do.

Then there is brushing your teeth
and combing your hair,
making sure never to get the two mixed up.

Then there is breakfast…. and finally off to school.

After school is finished it gets just as busy
with swimming classes, home to rush down tea…

and finally off to gymnastics.

Even after that it's still busy, with showers, stories, milk, brushing teeth and bed. Every Monday was always the same...

that is except for one particular Monday.

That particular Monday had started the same as any other but it all changed when Dad came home for tea.

Mum had cooked dinner for all of us
but Dad had been stuck in traffic so had to wait for his tea.

We were having sausages
for tea that night
and sausages were
one of Dad's favourites.

Mum had put his dinner on a plate and left it in the kitchen, which she normally did when Dad got stuck in traffic.

When Dad got home he was in for a bit of a surprise.
His sausages were gone!!!

Instead, all he had was a plate of broccoli, peas and lumpy mashed potato.
None of us knew where they had gone.

Chops quickly jumped on the case.
Putting on her detective outfit,
she tried to figure out where Dad's
sausages had gone.

First she questioned her brother to see if he had eaten them… he hadn't.

Then she questioned her Dad
to see if he was tricking her
and had actually eaten them already….

He hadn't.

Then she questioned her Mum to see if she had in fact cooked the sausages in the first place.... She had.

Nothing Chops did helped her uncover where the missing sausages had gone.

Chops turned to her detective kit
and pulled out her big purple magnifying glass.
She looked all around the kitchen
and suddenly found something
a little out of the ordinary.

It was a tiny gold bell...
and it had definitely fallen off of something small.

She continued to search the kitchen and was quickly surprised to find a small mound of squashed peas.

Not far from the squished pea pile was a sticky blob of gravy.

And after closer inspection, Chops found a trail
of gravy blobs leading right out of the back door.

The final blob of gravy looked decidedly like
a foot print, a small footprint, that is.

Chops followed the strange foot shapes
all the way through the garden to the trampoline
where they mysteriously disappeared.

Confused, Chops climbed up onto the trampoline for a quick bounce while she thought about what to do next.

All of a sudden after Chops completed her first big bounce, something dashed out from underneath the trampoline and disappeared up into the old wooden tree house.

Shocked, and a little afraid,
Chops chose to investigate the tree house.
She slowly crept up to the tree house,
pulled back the door and found....

Hairy the neighbour's fat cat.
All of a sudden it all made sense.
The sausage stealer
was in fact a cat...

a fat cat with
a missing bell
from its collar.

Chops ran back into the house to tell everyone what she had discovered.

Feeling sorry for the cat for having to steal food for its supper, Chops put out a big bowl of ice cream for it to have for its pudding.

And as for Dad… he had to settle for broccoli, peas and mum's lumpy mashed potato.

He didn't even get any ice cream
as Chops gave the last scoop to the fat cat burglar.

A short message about this book

Isabella was born in 2007 with a shortened left arm. It was only when she was born that we found out about her situation and as such, had many worries and concerns as to what she would and would not be able to do.

As it turns out, Isabella has been able to do everything she has chosen to do. She just finds her own way to do it - sometimes it's as we expect, other times it's a complete surprise.

This book is not a celebration of Isabella's achievements but a book that celebrates all children who have their own unique look and unique way of doing things.

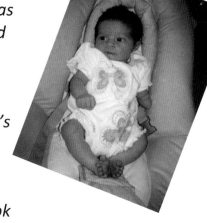

Thank you

for buying this book, we hope you enjoyed it.

There are many types of upper limb deficiency, it is so varied that getting support can be difficult. Reach hopes that by pooling the knowledge of its members it can offer support to all.

Isabella is proud to be a member of Reach... for more information on the organisation visit their website at reach.org.uk.

The Association for Children with Upper Limb Deficiency

32777080R00022